WONDER WOMAN

TEMPEST TOSSED

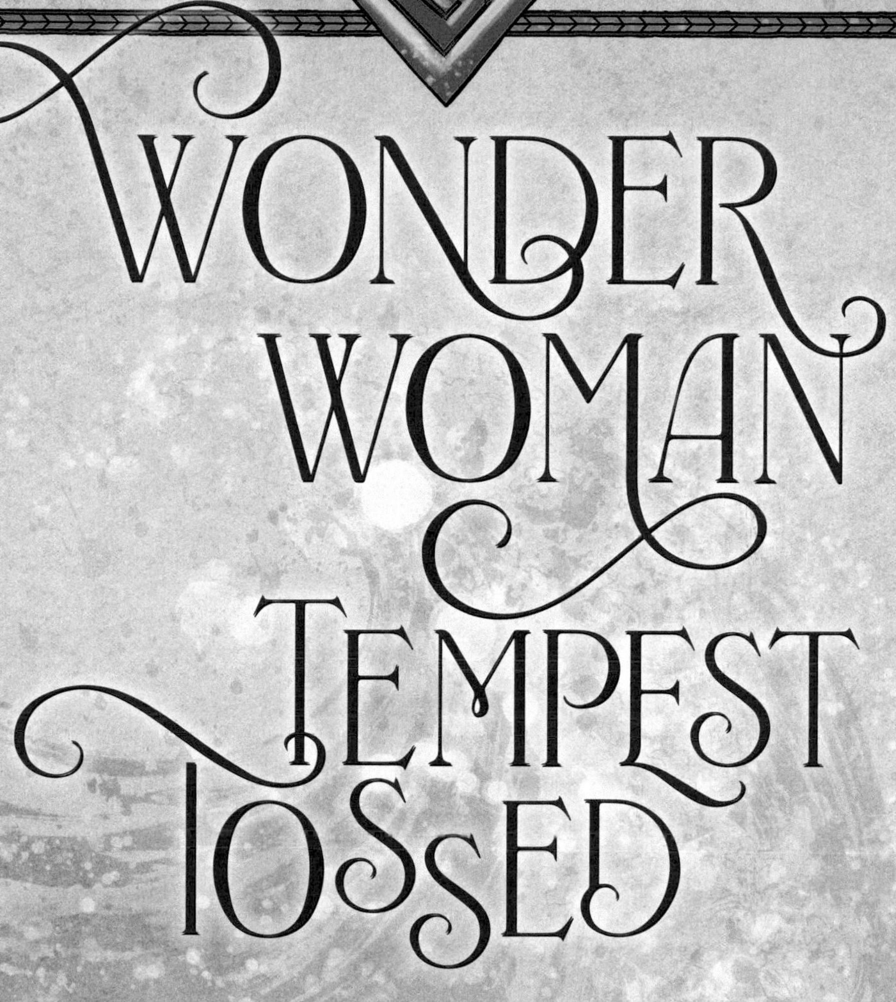

Laurie Halse Anderson Writer

Leila del Duca Artist

Kelly Fitzpatrick Colorist

Saida Temofonte Letterer

WONDER WOMAN: TEMPEST TOSSED

DC Comics, 2900 West Alameda Ave.,
Burbank, CA 91505
Printed by LSC Communications,
Crawfordsville, IN, USA. 4/24/20.
First Printing.
ISBN: 978-1-4012-8645-3

Library of Congress Cataloging-in-Publication Data

Names: Anderson, Laurie Halse, writer. | Del Duca, Leila, illustrator. | Fitzpatrick, Kelly, 1988- colourist. | Temofonte, Saida, letterer.
Title: Wonder Woman : tempest tossed / Laurie Halse Anderson, write Leila del Duca, illustrator ; Kelly Fitzpatrick, colorist ; Saida Temofonte, letterer.
Description: Burbank, CA : DC Comics, [2020] | Audience: Ages 13-17 Audience: Grades 10-12 | Summary: Princess Diana of Themyscira's birthday celebrations are cut short when refugees break through to h island home and she defies her Amazon elders by trying to bring the outsiders to safety, but a stormy sea sweeps her away to where she m learn to survive in a foreign world full of danger and injustice.
Identifiers: LCCN 2020009265 | ISBN 9781401286453 (paperback)
Subjects: LCSH: Graphic novels. | CYAC: Graphic novels. | Self-reliance--Fiction. | Justice--Fiction.
Classification: LCC PZ7.7.A476 Wo 2020 | DDC 741.5/973--dc23
LC record available at https://lccn.loc.gov/2020009265

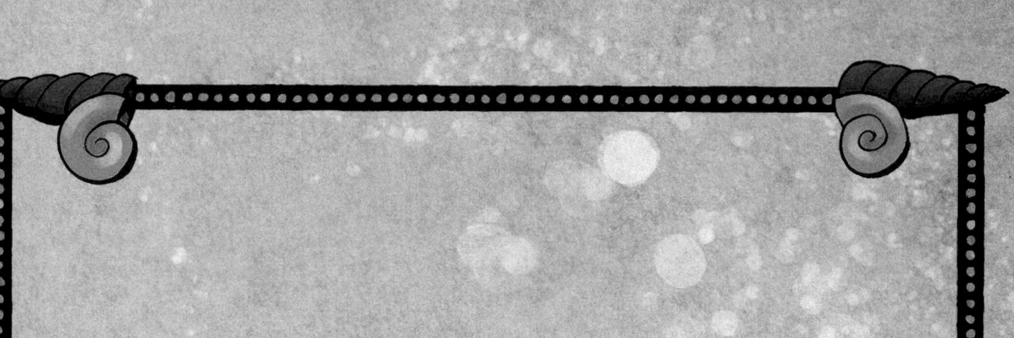

To my mother.

—Laurie Halse Anderson

To the countless refugees and asylum seekers who have risked everything for life, liberty, and the pursuit of happiness.

—Leila del Duca

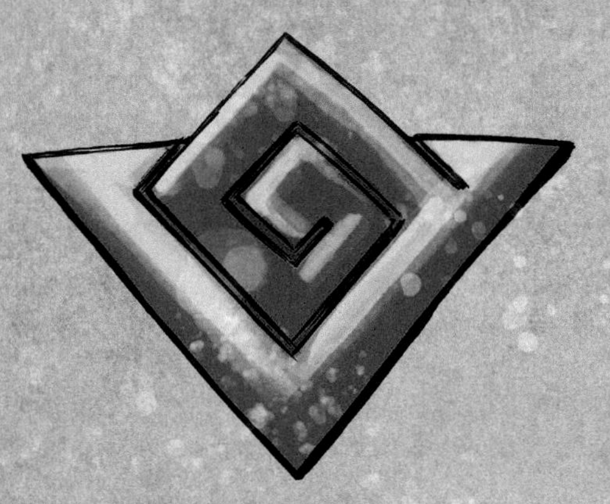

Themyscira. Secret island of the Amazons.
Home.
Safe from the outside world.
SKREE!
Home is the place where I belong.
Where we're family, good and strong.

HoOoCnk-shOo-hoOOOOOOOnCK

TWEET
CHEEP

Staaahp!
Ever wake up knowing it's a special day, but can't remember why?

And then it hits you?

This year has
een awful, but
now it's over.
Today I'm finally sixteen.
The healers warned you, Diana. Slow down!
By Athena's arrows, Phylonoe, I'm fine!
It's my Born Day!
May the Five Mothers help us.

At the dawn of time.
The Five Mothers gathered.
Athena.
Aphrodite.
Demeter.
Artemis.
Hestia.

hey gathered
o create the
Amazons—
—a race of
peace-loving
warriors—
—forged to
protect
the world.
The Mothers wove a barrier of
patience and time to shield
Themyscira from the outside.
The Amazons must stay
hidden here until the
Great Evil of the
Universe returns.
Then the Mothers
will summon them
to save humanity.
While they wait, the Amazons
have created a culture
based on love, strength,
and cooperation.

Sixteen years ago.

But the queen hungered for a child.

Finally, the Mothers granted her wish.

Me.

But in the last few years my body turned strange and unpredictable. The healers had never seen anything like it.
I grew as tall and fast as bamboo, but became clumsy and weak.
My moods hanged as ast as the weather.
They called me the Changeling.
Everyone promised the awful phase would end on my sixteenth Born Day.

Today.
I'm fine. Stop fussing.
You *must* visit the healers and the temple.
When will I get to see Mother?
I don't know. She's been out all night inspecting the barrier.
There are weak spots that need reweaving.
Has that ever happened before?
Not for a long time. But you have more important things to think about.
Many blessings on the day, Diana.

The marketplace.
Wishing you strength, Princess!
Happy Born Day!
Thank you!
I think I'm old enough to make my offerings on my own now.
I agree.
You do?
But the healers come first.
I'm so sick of them.
The queen insists. So do I.
You are both worry-worms. But I'll go.

The healer's compound.
Amazons heal fast and are nearly immortal.
Hello?
Since the healers don't have much work, they like observing me.
I'm their experiment.
They've been measuring and analyzing me since I was a baby.
CHANGELING
14
13
12
11
10
9
8
7
6
5
4
3
2
YEAR 1
I hate this place.
Princess Diana Year One
DIANA Year Two
DIANA Year Three
CHANGELING THEORIES
It makes me feel different, like I don't belong.
AMAZON
CHAN

Good morning, Princess.

Morning. Where is everyone?

They rode off with the queen last night.

Athena, grant me your wisdom. Help me be a good Amazon.

Aphrodite, grant me the beauty of a pure heart. Help me be a compassionate Amazon.

Demeter, grant me the strength of your Earth. Help me be a true Amazon.

Artemis, grant me the power of your hunt. Help me be a skilled Amazon.

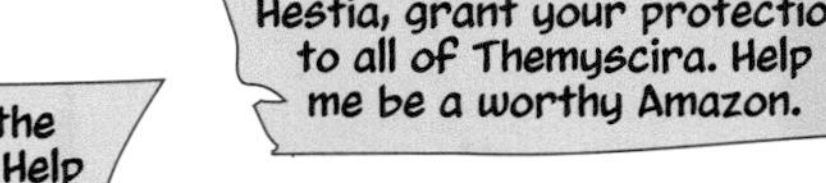

I feel it in my bones—the balance of earth and air, fire and water. Themyscira's powerful harmony.

They're here.

Please make me a real Amazon-powerful, good, and true. Make me strong again so I can fulfill my destiny.

Antiope has summoned you, Princess.
Phoof

The palace smithy.
Antiope is our general.

She's the strongest and most skilled warrior of all.

I want to be just like her.
Blessings and health, Princess!
Thank you.
REEEE

Good morning, Anti.
You look pale, hedgehog. Another bout of the weakness?

Nope! I feel great!
Good. Come see the new sword.

Remember when you thought swords were made in a day?

"Letting me try to make one was a good idea, Anti."
"You so wanted to prove me wrong. In the end, you fell asleep on the anvil."

Air feeds fire. Fire melts steel.
We beat out the weaknesses.

Takes a month to forge a sword, a lifetime to train a warrior. Ready to start?

The healers examined you, right? They've cleared you to train?
Antiope can smell a lie from the other side of the island.
They weren't ≠hunh≠ there. But I'm fine.
You truly think your days of weakness are over?
I am ready to train, Gene I swear it.

That's enough, child.

Nothing has changed.

I feel worthless.

There's no shame in feeling defeated.
All warriors deal with that.

I'm not a warrior. I'll ***never*** be one.
A sword's strength comes from the fire.

A warrior's strength begins in her heart.
Your strength is rising, hedgehog. I can feel it.
But-

I think this Born Day nonsense is foolish.
But sixteen years old deserves a present, they say.

Apples?
Freya likes apples best.

That's Freya. Your horse. Happy Born Day, Diana.

Oof!
You're giving me a *horse!*
Still have some strength left...

The queen and her riders approach. Open the gate!

"Mother looks terrible!"
"She carries heavy burdens, Diana."

Three holes in the barrier, all visible.
It's been a long time.
Holes? The outside world can see us?

Global war again?
And famine. Millions of refugees are fleeing.
They try to reach our neighbor's shores, from many different countries.

Wait— are we in danger?
You're too young for this, Diana. Go now.
No, my queen. She's old enough.

"When the nations outside battle each other, the barrier weakens.
"Their pain is so strong it reaches through our barrier.
"We can't help them until the Great Evil reveals itself.
"If we do, the worlds will go out of balance and destroy the universe."
A few mortals have landed on our shore in the past.
What did you–?
We gave them a forgetting tea, sent them away, and repaired the barrier.

But what if the Great Evil is returning?
Or if the mortals invade—

You're protected by an army of Amazons.
Don't worry, little one.

I'm not worried. I want to help!
Take Freya for a ride—she needs it.
Be back by sunset.

They don't think I'm old enough...
...or strong enough...

...they're wrong. Antiope said my strength is rising.
I'll show them.

I'll be the best warrior ever.
Aaaah!
WHOMP

The best at *failing.*

What if I'm stuck?

What if I'm a Changeling forever?

Deep in Hecate's Grove.

cHRRp
cHRRp
cHRRp

You're too little to be on your own.

CHPKA
CHPKA

cHRRp
cHRRp

Shhh.

Island creatures are natural-born...

...like this bird.

I wasn't. Maybe that's my problem.

What if I was a mistake?
KRAK
AAAAHH!
Ouch.

n hours later.

What in the name of the Five Mothers?

If I'm truly regaining my abilities, then Mother and Antiope will listen to me.

I'll *convince* them we should do more.

We should help the mortals.

Assuming I can survive the next five minutes.

I'm so sorry!

Anti, I climbed a huge tree and fell!
It knocked me out all day, but I saved a baby bird.
I was Amazon-strong and—
And the fall scrambled your wits?

Go on in. The queen is expecting you.
Gulp

HAPPY BORN DAY, PRINCESS!

I guess I'm not in trouble.
Happy Born Day, my dear daughter!

It is the best feast of my whole life.

The spirit of celebration carries us away from our troubles like a conjured ship of sails on the Ocean of Delight.
It takes me a while to realize who is missing...

Mother, where are the healers?
Still working on the barrier with the stargazers and godtalkers.
But enough about that–

Bring in the gifts!

Sixteen years ago the gods granted us the greatest gift of all—Diana, our princess.
Hurrah!
Yeesss!
TWE-TEWEEE!
TWEEE!

Our gifts pale next to that, but we hope they'll strengthen her as she grows into her power.
Phylonoe, the first box, please.

Gasp
May the Lasso of Truth help you find the knowledge that you seek from those who wish to hide it.

She's treating me like a proper princess!
Like an Amazon!
Hurrah! Hurrah!

May the Bracelets of Aegis protect your body and amplify your powers.
The lasso and bracelets warm me like a hug from an old friend.

May this crown forever mark you as the princess of the Amazons—

GONG GONG
GONG
Prepare!

Everything happens so fast, like a dream.

Empty rafts and footprints on the beach. More rafts at sea, near the barrier holes.
To arms!

Stay here!
No! I'm coming with you!
I command you to stay for your safety!

Not a dream.
A nightmare.

The Beach of Peisinoe.
I can't believe what I'm seeing.

Is that a...man? I've never seen one before.

‹They bombed our city. We have nowhere to live. Can you hear the children crying?›*
‹Quiet! You've broken our barrier.›
‹Please, help us!›
*Translated from Arabic.

THUMP

Gasp
That's enough.

This one's dead.
Light the funeral pyre as soon as possible. How many more?

A dozen adults ran to the forest, all carrying children.

Children?
The barrier is almost repaired. They must be off the island before that happens or else—
It's under control, my queen.

They have children?
Diana, I told you to stay at the palace.
‹Help us!›
‹Please, help!›

Send out the boats! They're *drowning!*
They're outside the barrier.
There is nothing we can do to help—you know that.

But the children can't swim!
‹Help! Help!›

They're *dying!*
The heat from my blood warms my bracelets...

The lasso squeezes my middle...
...encouraging me.

Go back to the palace *now!*
‹Please! Help us!›

Heart-strength pours through me.

Diana-no!
When the rules are wrong—

—you have to break them...

Especially when little ones are in trouble.
Mothers Five, keep the children alive.

It takes a long time to get everyone into a raft.
But as the dawn approaches...
...I'm ready to lead them to shore.
We'll give them supplies and forgetting tea, then send them on their way.

‹Please, Miss, get in the raft. You can't pull us for hundreds of miles.›
‹Don't worry! It's not far!›
The hole in the barrier was right here.

‹Where's the island? Can you see it?›

‹*What* island?›
‹*Themyscira!*›

‹My home...›

Somewhere in the Mediterranean.

Everyone is alive.

We're not alone.

But I'm trapped...

Outside.

Three days later. On a Greek island.
We made it to land.

Thirsty, hungry, and exhausted.
But alive.

I don't know what I was expecting—

—but it sure wasn't this.

Being lost on a stormy sea doesn't seem so bad right now.

‹Keep moving!›*
*Translated from Greek.

‹Let me help you. He wants us to keep walking.›*
‹How much farther is it?›
*Translated from Arabic.

I've never spoken to a man before. Are they as smart as women?
‹The children are tired. How much farther?›

‹Keep walking!›
Antiope would snap him in two. Mother would throw him into the sea.
But they're not here.

And I'm just a lost Changeling.

We're exhausted.

Everything is bewildering.

Is all of the Outside like this?
Waaaaaaa!
Mama!

‹Take what you need, then go through the door at the end of the hall for food.›*
I translate.
*Translated from Greek.

The clothes are for us. The next room has food for us.

You need these.
But...
Please—the guards can be dangerous.
I didn't think about that.
Th-thank you.

Pretend you can't speak their language.
Don't trust anyone.
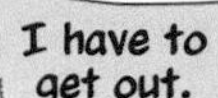
I have to get out.

This place is choking me.
I just want to go home.

But how?

Two weeks later...
Helping with the children makes me feel better.

But we waste hours a day waiting in lines—
—for food...

...paperwork...

...or the outhouse.

Some people have been stuck here for years.
But it's better than living in a war zone.
Gasp!
We're trapped and we can't leave.

She's not breathing!
‹Help! Help! Help! Help!›*
*Translated from four languages.

‹Let me go with her! She'll be afraid!›*
She needs to be with her daughter!
No pass. No go.
*Arabic.

They'll take good care of her.
Aaaaahhhhh!

I've got to make them understand.
Don't touch her!
‹That girl needs her mother!›*
‹What's wrong with you?›**
*Greek.
**Shawiya.

More men, more problems.
What's wrong?
They're trying to escape!

Who're you?
Steve Chang. My husband, Trevor and I work for the United Nations. We'r inspecting the camp.

The mom doesn't have papers.
Is paper more important than people? Are all of you ***monsters?***
Not all.

Don't worry, we'll be at the hospital soon.
UN

Hospital of Saint Ioannes.
Why is that vine growing from her?
Vine?
It gives her medicine.

How long can Kassandra stay?
Until Reema is better.

Thank you.
Thank *you.* Your translation really helped. Can we take you to lunch?

Steve and Trevor got us out of the camp.
Maybe they have other powers.
Even if they are men.

We'll eat and we'll talk.

Steve's a diplomat and Trevor's a doctor.
But mortals lie a lot. The camp taught me that.

They show me pictures of their work in orphanages, building schools, repairing houses, helping children.
I begin to believe them. A little.

Can you tell us about life in the camp?

I explain about the bad water, sick kids, families stranded for years—
—the lack of information, books, or real help.
Wars are terrible things.

You're different, Diana. Your hand is always close to a knife.
You scan your surroundings once a minute. Your evaluation of the camp was more professional than our staff gives.

Trevor was a Marine captain.
You act like a veteran tactical officer, but you're, what—fifteen years old?
Sixteen.

What languages did you speak at the gate?
English, Greek, and Shawiya.
That's... amazing.

You said you don't want to talk about your family or home-
But we want to help.
We suspect you have special talents.

My choices were the camp or...

U.S. embassy
...this place.
I told them the refugees need me, but they promised I could be more useful here.

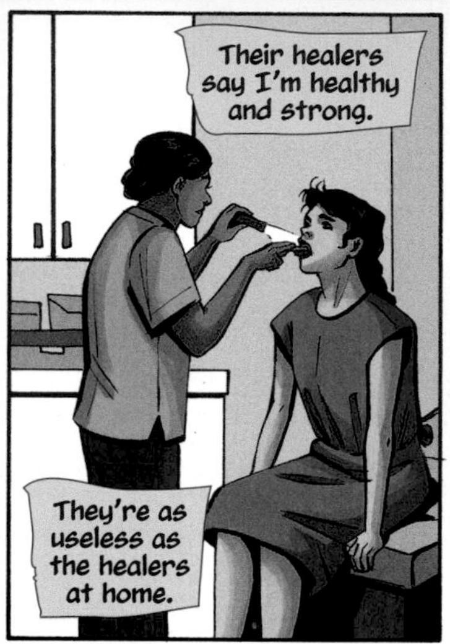
Their healers say I'm healthy and strong.
They're as useless as the healers at home.

I pass simple tests.

I can't tell if they are more surprised by what I know or what I *don't* know.
Let's move on to the languages...
WHA TO LEARN:
Biology
orld History
merican History
rative Religions
Literature
Economics
Computer Use
Life Skills
WHAT I KNOW:
Philosophy
The w of: Sappho
Ancient Greece
Aedesia
Hunting
Hypatia
Fishing
Aristoclea of Delphy

Apparently, mortals can't speak all of the languages like Amazons.
Maybe that's why they're always fighting.
Trevor and Steve have to go to emergency meetings at The Hague.*
*Home of the U.N.'s International Court of Justice, The Netherlands.
I read as much as I can...
...looking for clues about Themyscira...
...searching for ways to get home.

I hunt for weeks, but it's useless.

Mortals have no idea that Themyscira exists.

One week later.
We hate to say it, Diana...
...but it's time.
You must decide.

Come with us to America. We got you a three-year student visa. You can stay with my old assistant, Henke. She's wonderful.
Or you can take your chances and wait in the refugee center.
Sigh

But I don't want to leave the refugees behind.
You can help them more when you have a degree.
This is one of the hardest decisions of my life.

Help me, Mother.

On the morning of my Born Day...
...I thought my problems were over.
That I'd grown from Changeling to Amazon.
That I was ready to be a warrior.
Instead I lost everything.
Everyone.
I lost myself, too.
I am no one.

ew York City.
There she is—Lady Liberty.
She reminds me of Hestia.
Maybe that's a good sign.

John F. Kennedy Airport.
New York City.

Is this a temple?

It's J.F.K. airport.

Is J.F.K. the god of standing in line?

Pretty much.

Trevor got an emergency call and had to rush to the hospital.
I'm getting nervous about meeting their friend.

Okay. Tell me again: What's your story?

I'm an exchange student from Greece.
My parents died in a car accident.

You knew them in grad school.
Good.

Welcome to Queens
"The World's Borough"
A city named for queens is a good sign, too.

Henke Cukierek's apartment.

There you are!

Raissa! She's here!

You must be so hungry and tired!

Sorry, emergency council session. Gotta run!

Found her!

Raissa looks like a Changeling, like me.
Diana, this is my grand-daughter.
Erm, hello. Thank you for letting me stay with you.
Join us, Raissa.

Don't have time, Babciu.*
*Polish diminutive for grandmother.

Henke's look reminds me of Antiope.
Sit. My dear.

Raissa's parents are overseas this summer trying to free political prisoners.
What's a political prisoner?

Are you kidding?

‹Bad enough I'm stuck here, but I have to babysit?›
‹Those kids need me! She doesn't!›
‹Be polite!›
Should I tell them I speak Polish?

Raissa will show you Manhattan, Diana.
I have to work, Babciu.

KNOCK KNOCK
Get to know each other, girls!

I can't hang out with you. No offense.
Don't eat all the cookies.

I'm an intruder in the middle of a family civil war.
At least the food is good.

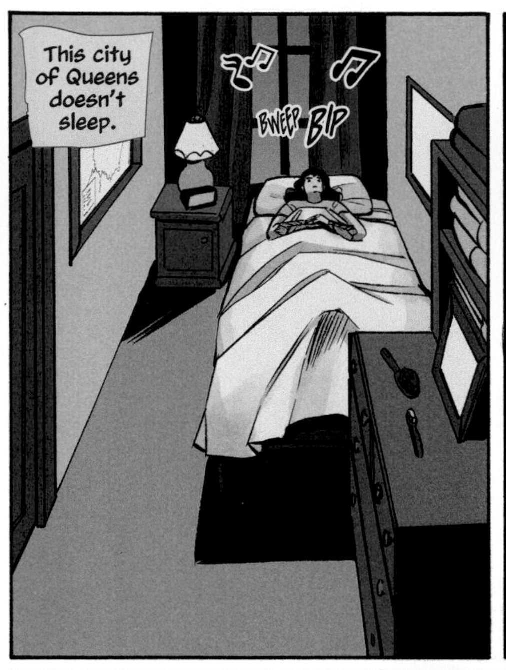
This city of Queens doesn't sleep.
BWEEP BIP

Mortals here turn night into day.
Hahaha! BWEEP
BOP
They erase the stars.

After dinner, Henke told me about working at the U.N., and how much she loves dancing. We didn't talk about Raissa.

I can't stop thinking of the smell of home— the sea, jasmine, and apricots.
Mother's perfumed oils, Antiope's sweaty hair, Phylonoe's soap.

I must put the past away.

Next morning. Finally.
Get dressed. You have to come with me.
But—

SLAMM
Morning, dragon breath.

Uncle Steve sent you some clothes.
I have clothes.
Whatever.

SLAMM
POLAND

Finally. I make lunch for neighborhood kids.
My friends bailed today. I can't carry everything on my own.

Can I help?
Duh.

HOOONK
Slow down!
Welcome to the Big Apple!
$
Are you okay, ma'am?
She's sleeping. I'll explain it while we walk.
But she's sleeping on the sidewalk!

Hooocnk-shoo

Peanut butter and jelly won't go bad in the heat.
But she can't stay—
Come. I'll explain.

Raissa explains about America's homeless people. They sound like refugees in their own country.
You did the right thing back there.
Thank you.

Don't you have homeless people where you're from?
None.
Wish I could see that.

Wheetwheeew!
Gimme that sweet candy, baby!

Are they hunting? Whistling for their dogs?
Ha. They think they're hunting us, but—
Hunting us?

Grrrrr...

That's!
Not!
Nice!

Whoa! Diana, we're good!
Put down the trash!

That how you deal with jerks at home?
My aunts would have killed those jerks.
Your aunts would love Babciu.

Sorry I was a bitch earlier.
Sorry I messed up your plans.

I hate this summer.
It sucks.

What's that smell?

They never pick up the garbage on this street.

HAVE YOU SEEN THIS GIRL?
It smells like death.
Probably rotting cheese. Come on.

Let me show you something nicer...

Elizabeth Freeman Park.
Welcome to the heart of the neighborhood!
It's *paradise!*
We think so.
Elizabeth Freeman Park

I love this park!

Want to play?
Yes!

Maybe you should slow—

Ha-hahaha!
Heh-heh-heh!
Hee-hee-hee-hee!

Baby mortals are fascinating.
She likes you.

She's a miracle.

Hey! A little help?

Parents around here work two or three jobs.
It's still not enough to pay the bills.

Schools offer free lunches, but not in the summer.

I wanted to help, but I'm only seventeen.
So what did you do?

I made lunch.

Babciu and her friends pay for the food. The churches help, too.

Raissa is cranky when she wakes up...
Join us!
...but she has a good heart.

No thanks. We're looking for a girl.
Kristen Liu? From the posters?
No, our babysitter. Celena.

She disappeared from her group home two nights ago. The lady who runs it doesn't care. The cops won't tell us anything.
We can't believe she'd run away like that. Something has to be wrong.

We'll keep an eye out for her.
Thanks. Here's our number.

Why would anyone run away from home?
Not all homes are safe.

I can't imagine what it's like to live in a home that isn't safe.

No!

‹Don't cry, it's okay. Here, take mine.›
‹Thank you!›

You speak Sudanese?

Ayen speaks Dinka, not Sudanese Arabic.
You can speak *Dinka?!*

Um... a little.

BWOONK
Yikes, that's loud.

AAAAAAAH!
Why are they so upset?
They're just playing. It's nothing.

Stay here. I gotta talk to my friends.
Can't I meet them?
Not right now. Just stay put, okay?

<The trash truck?>

<They steal children. Girls.>

I haven't spent much time around kids...

...but I think she's telling the truth.

‹Raissa will know what to do.›
‹She's really smart about this world.›

The trash men are stealing children!

Guys, this is Diana. She's new.
We need to tell the police, right?

Kids love to scare themselves with stories about the bogeyman.

You're not taking this seriously.
It's just a *story*. A *game*.

Back off.
Excuse me?

You need to leave.
Are you always this rude?
Just go, guys. I'll see you tonight.

Why are you being so annoying?
I was just—
Shut up!

We didn't talk after that.

Hunh
Hunh

There are two casseroles in the freezer and ice cream for dessert. Don't Wait up!!
COLOR

How am I supposed to cook this?

Being able to speak a language is different from really understanding it.

It's all very confusing.

I keep having the same dream...
...but tonight something wakes me.
You got everything?
Raissa?
Don't want to get caught again.
You worry too much.
Raissa doesn't worry enough.
That's my job.

Where are they going?
Why would she sneak out like this?
Why did I sneak out?
Mothers Five!

Hahahah!
My aunts would cheer these strange games.

If mortals can...

Okay. Nice start.
Not quite Amazon standards...
...but good enough.

One hour later...
I'd have been better than anyone before I was a Changeling.

Diana!

How'd you find us?
You okay?

I followed you.

Not cool. You weren't invited.
Be nice, Beck. She's still learning.

Well, you should teach her better.
Hey! What's your problem?

Sorry. She needs some sleep.
We'll call you later, Ray.
I just wanted to make sure you were safe.
That was a dumb, but sweet, thing to do. Thanks.
I can't believe you tried this. It's a beast.
I fell.
Falls don't matter. Getting up does.
You hungry?

I thought people ate at restaurants.
Not trucks.
AN FEAST
GREEK

Your island doesn't have food trucks?
Ahhh... not yet.

NIGERIAN FEAST
Four meat pies, four coffees.
Please.

We need to document this!

500 LUXURY UNITS COMING SOON!
CONDO PALACES OF QUEENS! DRYGION L.L.C.

We gonna make lunch?
Thursdays are the Baptist church's turn. We get to chill.

Shhh. We don't want to wake up Babciu.
Why not?

Where have you been?
Getting breakfast for you, Babciu!

I was afraid you snuck out again.
To jump off buildings or other crazy things.

No, ma'am. Not us.
You're lying, of course.

And your punishment is coming with me to polka.
Oh god, no!
What's *pull*-kuh?

Later, at the community center.
LADIES
CHANGING ROOM
This way, girls!
Raissa's reaction made me think that "polka dancing" was torture. I was wrong.
This is the best!
Kill me now.

We get to spend the whole day here!

I convinced Raissa to dance.

This dance reminds me of one we perform after the summer wheat is planted on Themyscira.
Must be a coincidence.

Hours later.
The lines in the elders' faces are like maps of their lives.

That's Emil. She's helping him study for his naturalization test. Cute, right?
Beautiful.

Last one, please. Think of it as parkour training in a pretty dress.

Dancing polka could bring worldwide peace.
Do you know how weird you are?

Next morning.
Uncle Steve promised a day of adventure.
He's here!

Bye!
Later, Henke!

Why isn't Raissa coming?
Not quite.
She's grounded. Is it a housekeeping ritual?

What's down here—a cellar?
The subway—it's an underground train.
Trains run under the *ground?*
Thought you'd like it.
E F

Trevor sends his love. He's back in Greece.
Refugees keep arriving there, needing doctors.

LEARN
English at night!
I, Too
Langston Hu
Is it the war?

Wars, plural. Another one broke out last week.

CIVILIAN MASSACRE. CHOLERA OUTBREAK. CHILD TRAFFICKING ON THE RISE.

United Nations Headquarters, New York City.
Welcome to the United Nations, Diana!
Delegates come here from all over the globe.
We're trying to end suffering and promote peace.

Why not just stop the wars? Help all the refugees and feed the hungry children?
Sigh

It's complicated.
Excuse me, Mr. Chang.
Pardon me, Diana...

Themyscira's delegate would sit there...
Thailand
Timor-Leste

...if the world knew about us.
Ready to see more?

Official languages of the United Nations: Arabic, Chinese, English, French, Russian, and Spanish.
Language interns study here after college.
Translating in the General Assembly?

We have projects all over the world that need translators.
You'd be great. With your talent, you could work anywhere.

I should learn how to get through spinning doors first.
Won't take long.

Later, in Central Park.
So how are you adjusting?
There's lots of slang to learn.

American culture confuses me. How do some people own many houses, while others sleep on sidewalks?
Got any easier questions?
So many!!

Why is the bogeyman funny?
How can anyone be racist?
Why does some coffee taste great and other coffee horrible?
Why don't people just share everything?
Why do they call New York "the Big Apple"?
Why do you look so tired?

Steve promised I could go to a school in the fall—one that would help me find the answers I want.
For the next month, I focus on training.

Wow—you learn fast!

Brava!
I get stronger every day.
And Raissa becomes more of a friend.

We talk about Changeling things like face pox and moonbleeding.
Paper sticks? Not moss?
Yep.

The best part is the children.

Does it seem like we have more kids today?

What can we do?
Ummm...

The little ones are smarter than we are.
But we still need more food.

We explain to the food truck owners about the extra kids we can't afford to feed.

Good luck!
They promise to help as often as they can.
GREEK

Raissa convinces the library to hold story time in the park.

Some kids are so burdened by hard things.
I wish I could make life fair and joyful for all of them.

Remember the babysitter who ran away?
Celena?
Your memory is scary good. Yes, Celena.

Did the moms find her? Is she okay?

Nope. Still missing.

The moms asked Social Services to investigate.

Lots of kids ran away from group homes this summer. But there's not enough staff to track them down.
Maybe Henke can help.

Morning!

Hello, Henke!

Together we collect honey, make cider, and dry fish. We share the work and the food.
I miss it.
I was homesick when I first got here, too.
I was born in Poland. When I was your age, our democracy movement was outlawed.
Thousands were beaten and jailed for protesting.
Including me.

I immigrated here when I got out of jail.

Heard about the new condos down the block, Henke?
We need new schools, not condos.

Bad group homes are a bigger problem than condos, Babciu.

Raissa explains about Celena as we finish shopping.

No one cares that she's missing! She's trapped on a...on a...on a merry-go-round from hell!

Not a merry-go-round, dear. The poor child is trapped in the cycle of poverty.
I'll make some calls, see what I can find.
I'll get more eggs.

What's a merry-go-round?

It looks like a strange American version of Aphrodite's temple.

You crack me up. Come on!

And it just goes around in a circle?

Aha! A *fast* circle! I love it!
Right?!

Are you okay, Sofia?
My tummy hurts.

Hrrrk!

Want to sit down?

She okay?
Yep.

But I don't understand this—child trafficking? How can kids make traffic? Crowding the swing set?

Child trafficking is modern slavery. Kids and teens are kidnapped or lured by bad guys, then forced to work.
Doing what?
Picking crops or smuggling, but mostly...

...they're forced to have sex.

Ever smell evil in the air, or feel like bad things are getting close?

Like a goose stepping on your grave?
A creepy chill?

We say the gods are warning us when we get this feeling of... badness.

The gods are whispering, but I can't hear what they're saying.

Next morning...
Sure you're okay? You look like hell.
Couldn't sleep.

Still thinking about Celena?
How can everyone just go on with their lives when kids are missing?

Babciu's friend in Social Services promised to investigate.
What if she's too late? Isn't there something else we can do?

All right. Follow me.

No offense, but...
...let me do the talking, okay?

Sure.

The officer asks lots of questions. We don't have many answers.
Defeating evil is harder than I thought.
GROCERY & DELI

Those girls have become a real pain in the ass.
We gotta tell the boss.

Next day.
Are you Raissa Cukierek?
Raissa Díaz Cukierek. Can I help you?
Something's not right.

Where are your permit and Food Safety Certification?
Why?
Just answer the question.

Not against the law to have a picnic, is it?
You've got at least fifty sandwiches in here.

I like sandwiches. I can eat a lot of them.

You've broken at least thirty ordinances.
It's just a picnic.

Hey!
You can't do that!

You're a monster! A heartless troll!
I got this, Diana. Go hang with the kids.

Can I see some I.D., please?
Something is very wrong.

I want to punch brick walls. Drop a skyscraper on those fools.
That bad feeling is back, the sense that evil is close.
I want...
...to explode.
Don't touch her!

Did you hear me?
Get lost, kid.

Diana, no!

FWSHHHH

KRSCHK!

Don't hurt her!
THUNK

You have the right to remain silent...
SSNAP

What just happened?

I can't hear what he's saying.
I just hear buzzing, like I'm trapped in a beehive.

Maybe I cracked my skull when I fell out of that tree on my Born Day.

Maybe I'm *dead.*

Twelve hours later, Central Booking.

That illegal now?
I broke a picnic table, too.
I wanted to do that once.

Dinner is served.

SHOUT 4 JUSTICE!
RELEASE THE KRAKEN!
SO ANNOYING
NO MEANS NO
YES!
HONEY DEW

Anybody want this?

SHOUT 4 JUSTICE!
where am I?
MY LAWYER SUX
Thanks!

Tempered by fire, by the hammer, by water.

Themyscira has no jails.

Here they don't have swords or justice.
Or peace.

I've been lost since my Born Day. I don't belong anywhere.

I am a badly forged girl, filled with mistakes and easily broken.

Help me, Mothers, please.

Diana Prince? Your uncle bailed you out.

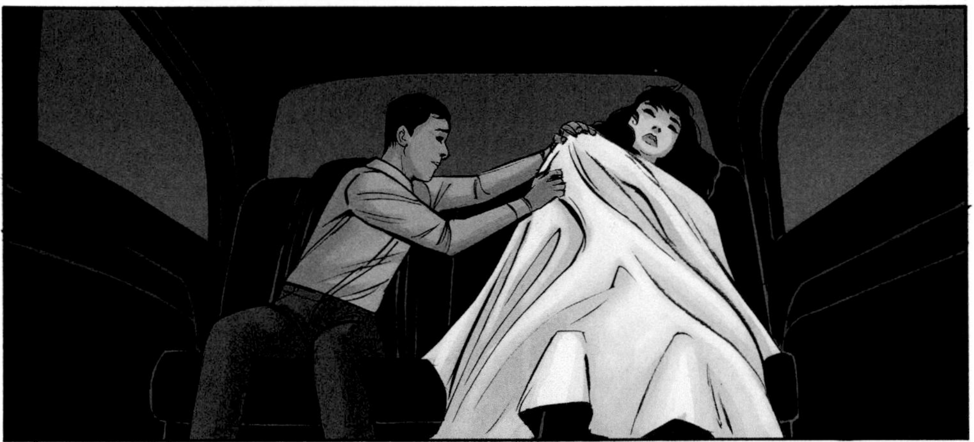

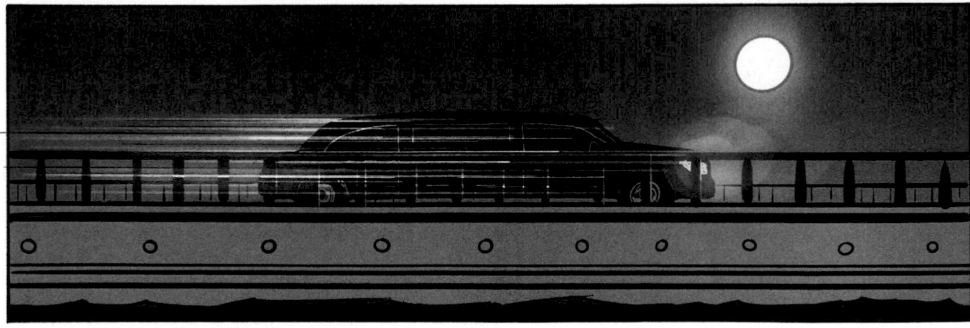

Two hours later...
Welcome to paradise. My family came here every summer when I was a kid.

My cousin still lives in the house back there.

It's a good place to clear your head.

And go for a swim.

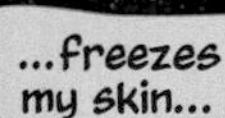

...chills my bones...

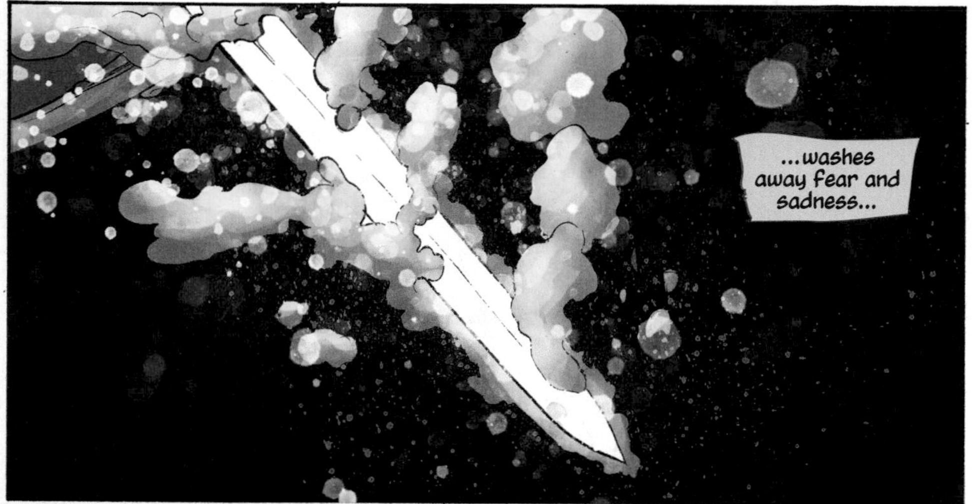
...washes away fear and sadness...

...and strengthens my courage.

The salt sea reminds me whose daughter I am.

The charges will be dropped. Don't worry.

Steve is kind and he means well...
All teens do dumb things. When I was your age...

...but I stop listening to him after a while.
Blah, blah-blah, blahing, super-blah...

I begin to listen to my heart.

Next day.
BALTIC SEA
POLA
Knock knock! May I come in?
Of course.

BALTIC SEA
I had a long talk with Steve this morning—
ND
I'm sorry, Henke.

I'll pack my things...

...and leave.

You want to leave us?
I don't *want* to leave, but... I was arrested. I shamed you.

I'm just glad Steve got you out!

All teens make mistakes.
I'm a Changeling, not a teenager.

You are my friend and this is your home.

Anybody hungry?

POLAND
Emil needs a suit for his citizenship ceremony. Want to come shopping?
Nope! We have a meeting at the library.

Okay, my Changelings—but after the meeting, you come straight home.
We—
—promise.

A meeting?
The city shut down our lunch program because our paperwork was wrong. We gotta figure out what to do next.

I can't eat this. Not with hungry kids down the street.

Oh. Good point.

School starts in a few weeks. Kids will be fed there.
I still don't understand why any child has to go hungry.

We'll change that, you and me. But first— the library.

Temperature's dropping—bring a hoodie!

Sorry—I used slang again. "Hoodie" means sweatshirt.

Wow! Where'd you get those?
IMMIGRATI
BUILT
THIS NATI

Birthday present from my auntie.
Awesome!

Let's go.

It could have been Henke's comforting words...
...or the swim in the sea or being freed...
...or all of it, but I feel amazing.
IMMIGRATION BUILT THIS NATION
Amazon amazing.

VIVLIA STREET PUBLIC LIBRARY

You have libraries like this on your island?

Our library is a bit bigger. But this is nice!
COMICS/GRAPH
SEEKING
ASYLUM
IS A
HUMAN

Sorry we're late.
OPTIONS:
IMMIGRATION BUILT THIS NATION
SEEKING ASYLUM IS A HUMAN RIGH

We're just getting started. Sonia?

The health inspectors who confronted Raissa were impostors, but the city caught wind of our lunch program and sent a cease and desist letter.
And it gets worse.

Drygion Corp. is about to destroy our community.

OPTIONS

Drygion is the shitty company that tried to steal our park.
OPTIONS:
-CITY HALL PROTEST
-ALERT MEDIA

OPTIONS:
-CITY HALL PROTEST
-ALERT MEDIA
DRYGION:
-DONATIONS/BRIBESTO CITY COU
-THREATS
-SUPREME COURT APPEAL
They want to gentrify the neighborhood and push out working-class families.

TAP
TAP

Go ahead. It's gonna be a long meeting.
IMMIGRATION BUILT THIS NATION

Ayen!
ASYLUM
IS A
HUMAN RIGHT

This is my mother, Munira, and my sister, Nyaring.
It's a pleasure to meet you. I am Diana.
Can you help her with some papers?

Every time we submit our asylum application, they demand more information.
SEEKING
ASYLUM
IS A
HUMAN RIGHT

It took a while, but we finally finished Munira's application.
Mortal governments worship paperwork, it seems.

Three hours later...
The library is closing in ten minutes.

For a moment I was so deep in the story, I forgot where I was. It was a nice break.
WAR AND PEACE
War and Peace

You looked so peaceful.
This place is like an island.
Great description!

Ready?
IMMIGRATION BUILT THIS NATION

What's the plan?
We could only agree that we needed another meeting.

CLICKK

There must be *something* we can do.
You don't get it, do you?

Drygion has all the money and power.
We have nothing. And don't go all *Optimism Girl* on me.
I can't deal with it, not tonight.
IMMIGRATION BUILT THIS NATION

Let's just go home.

What the—?
Hey! Who's in charge here?
IMMIGRATION BUILT THIS NATION
Maybe we should—
Record this on your phone. It's gonna get ugly.
I left my phone in Steve's car.
Go home, girls.

Use mine.
IMMIGRATION BUILT THIS NATION

This is a public park!
City sold it. Drygion's building condos here.

DDDT-
DDDT-

You're not as smart as your parents, Raissa...
DDDT-DDDT-DDDT-
DRYGION L.L.C.
CHIP DRYGION,
J.D., M.B.A. C.E.O.
Master of Enterprise
Carter Building
Lyndan Heights,
NY 10577

...or as crafty as your grandmother. You're a little girl having a temper tantrum.

Our lawyers will file cease and desist orders within the hour, Drygion.

I dare you to try.
SEEKING ASYLUM IS A HU AN R

It's time, Boss.
We'll have to continue this later. I'll send flowers to your grandmother, Raissa. I remember where she lives.

Did you hear that?
The threat? Absolutely. I hope the phone got it.
Diana!

Munira?

They took Ayen!

<I saw a man pull Ayen into a van.>*
Someone in a van drove off with Ayen.
What kind of van?
SEEKING ASYLUM IS A
*Translated from Dinka.

The trash men! I'll follow the truck!

Wait! Has she called the police?
Yes, but they said it's too soon.
We'll call them, make them understand it's an emergency.

I'll find her! I promise!
Where are you going?
SEEKING ASYLUM IS A HUMAN RIGHT

Diana! Wait!
SEEKING ASYLUM IS A

I called ⥼hunh⥽ the cops.
'Member how afraid Ayen was of the trash men? It's all connected. We'll find her if we follow the truck.
Good.

What are you doing?

Get down!
I need to get higher to spot the truck!

Found it!

Three blocks straight ahead! On the right!
I'll call the police! Please be—

-careful.

It smells evil.

By the Mothers!
Alive, but where's Ayen?

I thought we had another week.

Boss says move? We move 'em.

You sure the drugs will keep them asleep?

They'll be out cold the whole night.

Ayen!

Wait— we're missing one.
Shut up. You can't count that high.

I can hide her in the back, but...

Damn—
you're right.
Took out four,
got twenty
left.
You're
such an
idiot.

How come
we gotta do all
the carrying?
Cuz they
told us to,
dumbass.

How long
should
I wait?
And where
are the
other
drivers?

An hour later...

Get her!

C'mere, you—

POW
Aahhh!

Oww!

PING
PING

How?!

Ughh!

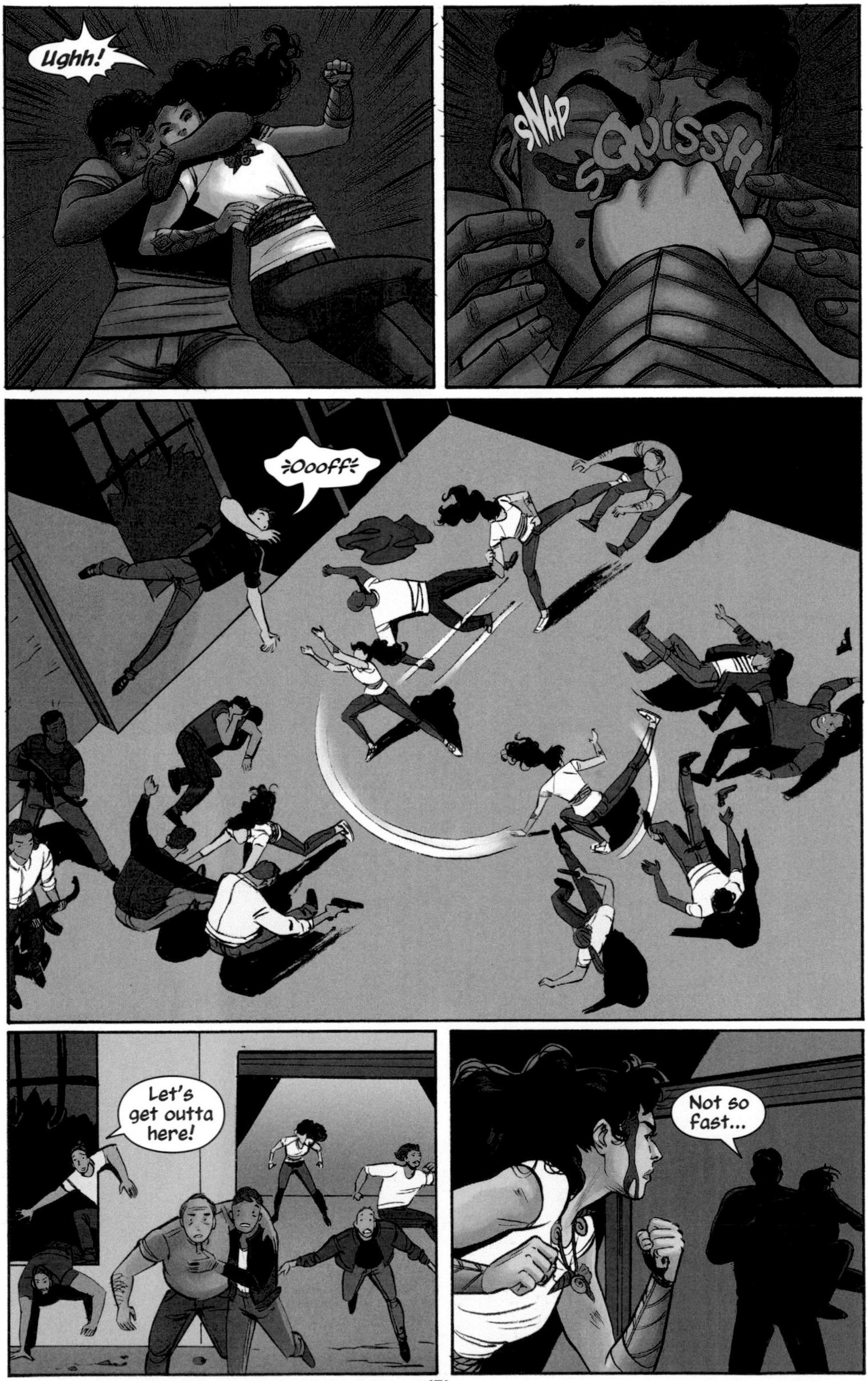

SNAP
SQUISSH

Oooff

Let's get outta here!

Not so fast...

You have my attention, young lady. There's more to you than meets the eye.
Drygion! Of course! He's even more evil than we knew...
Run, Diana!

Ahhhh!
Stop! Don't hurt her!

At first I thought we'd ship you with the rest of the product.

But then I saw you in action.

I could use someone with your talents.
Let Raissa go and I'll do anything you want.
Put your hands up.

If the brat moves, I'll shoot her. If you move, I will shoot her. Got it?
Yes.

WHOMP WHOMP WHOMP WHOMP WHOMP
Helicopter coming.
Time to leave, I suspect.

WHOMP WHOMP
Ooof

I'm fine! Don't let them get away!
Oh no you don't!
RAAAH!
NYP

NYPD
WHOMP WHOMP WHOMP WHOMP WHOMP
Where is my daughter?

Is she okay?

I think so. They drugged the kids to make it easier to smuggle them out of the city.

I don't think they had time to... hurt her.

One hour later...
When can we go home?
Not until Babciu gets here. She's probably dancing with Emil and can't hear her phone.
IMMIGRATION BUILT THIS NATION

She's so going to kill us.

Seriously?
It's a peak selfie moment! Wish I took pics when you went all badass in there.

Then the police would have to believe me.
The bad guys ran because the police showed up.
You threw their cars in the air.
You're hallucinating, Raissa. Probably have a concussion.

Two weeks later, main branch of the New York Public Library.
When they find him, Drygion is going to prison for a long time—child trafficking, bribery, tax evasion, money laundering, illegal trash dumping...
If they find him.
When.

Cursed be his name, dead be his bones.

Looks more like a temple than a library.

Just don't spit in here.
Shush, girls. And put away that phone!

"I hereby declare, on oath...

"...that I will support and defend the Constitution and laws of the United States of America...

"...against all enemies, foreign and domestic...

"...so help me God."

To celebrate, Emil is taking all of us to the Statue of Liberty.
STATUE OF LIBERTY FERRY

We brought snacks!
Cookies and oranges, but not cotton candy.
Smart choice.

You feel okay? Any lingering achiness? Nightmares?
I'm fine, Dr. Trevor.
I've never seen anyone recuperate like you.
Must have been born under a lucky star.

She looks like Hestia.
Friend of yours?

Sort of. She's the goddess of family and the home.
I think she looks like Henke.
All I'm missing is a crown.

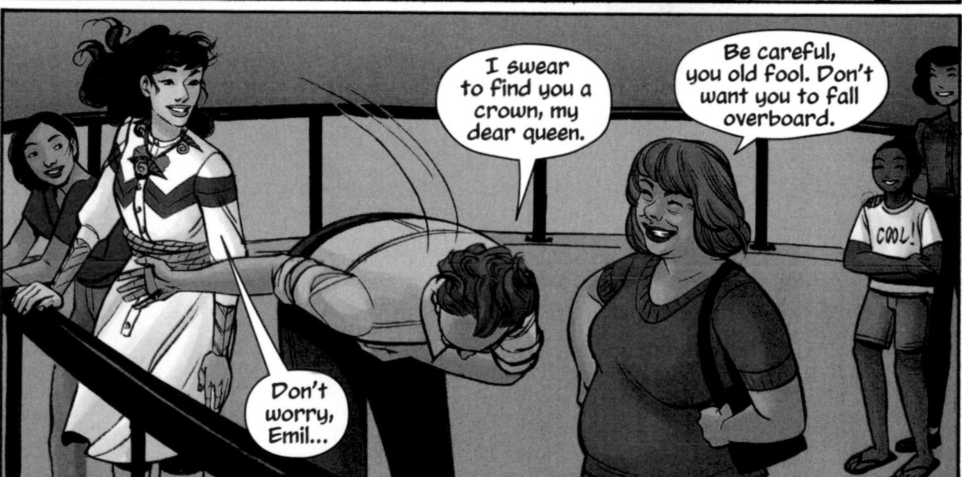
I swear to find you a crown, my dear queen.
Be careful, you old fool. Don't want you to fall overboard.
Don't worry, Emil...
COOL!

...if you fall in the water, I'll rescue you. I'm good at it.

THE NEW COLOSSUS.

NOT LIKE THE BRAZEN GIANT OF GREEK FAME,
WITH CONQUERING LIMBS ASTRIDE FROM LAND TO LAND;
HERE AT OUR SEA-WASHED, SUNSET GATES SHALL STAND
A MIGHTY WOMAN WITH A TORCH, WHOSE FLAME
IS THE IMPRISONED LIGHTNING, AND HER NAME
MOTHER OF EXILES. FROM HER BEACON-HAND
GLOWS WORLD-WIDE WELCOME; HER MILD EYES COMMAND
THE AIR-BRIDGED HARBOR THAT TWIN CITIES FRAME.
"KEEP, ANCIENT LANDS, YOUR STORIED POMP!"
CRIES SHE
WITH SILENT LIPS. "GIVE ME YOUR TIRED, YOUR
POOR,
YOUR HUDDLED MASSES YEARNING TO BREATHE FREE,
THE WRETCHED REFUSE OF YOUR TEEMING SHORE.
SEND THESE, THE HOMELESS, TEMPEST-TOST TO ME,
I LIFT MY LAMP BESIDE THE GOLDEN DOOR!"

Pretty cool, huh?

Awesome.

1849 1887

EMMA LAZARUS

Once, all the immigrants coming to New York City had to stop at Ellis Island.
Did you?

No, dear. That was a few years before my time.

Let's keep an eye on the clock. The ferry leaves soon.

Who wants to go to the gift shop?
I do!
I do!
I do!

Quite a view, right?

It could use a beach.
Good point.

Someday we'll have a penthouse apartment over there with a view of this statue.

Wait— we?

Of course! You're my sistergirl!
Soon we'll go to college, then we get to change the world.

I haven't thought that far ahead.
Maybe it's time to start.

Maybe it is.

Let's go, girls.
I'll be down in a sec.
For the first time, I think about a future here.
And while I'll never stop trying to find my family...
...and Drygion...
...or help the refugees and children...

...the Outside is my world now.
The place where I belong.
Where I have family, good and strong.
SKREE
My new home.

Naturalization Oath of Allegiance to the United States of America

"I hereby declare, on oath, that I absolutely and entirely renounce and abjure all allegiance and fidelity to any foreign prince, potentate, state, or sovereignty, of whom or which I have heretofore been a subject or citizen; that I will support and defend the Constitution and laws of the United States of America against all enemies, foreign and domestic; that I will bear true faith and allegiance to the same; that I will bear arms on behalf of the United States when required by the law; that I will perform noncombatant service in the Armed Forces of the United States when required by the law; that I will perform work of national importance under civilian direction when required by the law; and that I take this obligation freely, without any mental reservation or purpose of evasion; so help me God."

RESOURCES

If you are in immediate danger, please call emergency services in your area (9-1-1 in the U.S.) or go to your nearest hospital emergency room.

If you suspect that someone might be in need of help, contact the National Human Trafficking Hotline to connect with services and support for human trafficking survivors, or to report a tip, call 1-888-373-7888, text 233733, or chat online at https://humantraffickinghotline.org.

FOR MORE INFORMATION

International Rescue Committee
The International Rescue Committee helps people whose lives and livelihoods are shattered by conflict and disaster to survive, recover, and regain control of their future.
https://www.rescue.org

The Polaris Project
Founded in 2002, Polaris is named for the North Star, which people held in slavery in the United States used as a guide to navigate their way to freedom. Today they are filling in the road map for that journey, and lighting the path ahead.
https://polarisproject.org

Safe Horizon
The largest provider of comprehensive services for domestic violence survivors and victims of all crime and abuse including rape and sexual assault, human trafficking, stalking, youth homelessness, and violent crimes committed against a family member or within communities. If you need help, call their 24-hour hotline at 1-800-621-HOPE (4673) or visit safehorizon.org.

Laurie Halse Anderson is a *New York Times* bestselling author known for tackling tough subjects with humor and sensitivity. Two of her books, *Speak* and *Chains*, were National Book Award finalists, and *Chains* was also short-listed for the United Kingdom's Carnegie Medal. She was selected by the American Library Association for the Margaret A. Edwards Award for her significant contribution to young adult literature. Laurie has also been honored for her battles for intellectual freedom by the National Coalition Against Censorship and the National Council of Teachers of English. She is a member of RAINN's National Leadership Council and frequently speaks about sexual violence.

Leila del Duca is a comic book creator based in Portland, Oregon. Besides drawing *Wonder Woman: Tempest Tossed*, she has drawn *Sleepless* and *Shutter* and wrote *Afar* at Image Comics. Leila has also worked on titles such as *The Wicked + The Divine*, *Scarlet Witch*, *American Vampire*, and *The Pantheon Project*. During her spare time, she loves to make food, read, dabble in music, and do craft projects, especially during the Portland rainy months. She also loves staring off into space and considers it her favorite pastime.

In ***You Brought Me the Ocean***, by Lambda Award-winning author **Alex Sanchez** (*Rainbow Boys*) and *New York Times* bestselling illustrator **Julie Maroh** (*Blue Is the Warmest Color*), Jake Hyde must balance the future everyone expects for him against the one that's calling to his heart. His search for truth in this coming-of-age romance will reveal not only newfound powers, but also a new understanding of himself.

Read on for a special sneak preview of *You Brought Me the Ocean.*

On sale June 9, 2020.

So, you hike often?
All the time—with Maria. Do you hike much?
WELCOME TO TRUTH OR CONSEQUENCES
Naw, I'm more of a water guy—swimming, kayaking, white-water rafting.
You ever try it?
I'd love to, but my ma's scared of me getting near water—except to drink it.
Funny thing is, I'm always thirsty. I guzzle at least three gallons a day.
Maria teases me about it.
So, is Maria your girlfriend?
Or your girl friend?

She's my **best** friend.
I love her, but not **that** way.
Right now we're deciding where to go to college.
I'm hoping to go to my dream school—Miami.
She wants to stay closer to home.
BEWARE
FLASH FLOOD
Does she know about you?
Um, know what about me?
Relax. I'm not going to out you.

I...I've never told anyone.
There's always a first time.

When did you first tell other people about you?

In middle school I told my friend Gillian.

She already suspected—no big shocker.

Yeah, Maria probably knows. She should know—
She knows everything else about me.

Maybe she knows but doesn't want to see it.

You think Maria's got a **crush** on me?

The way you two are always together...
I figured you were a couple. Maybe she does, too.

But she and I are so different!
And it's not like I've ever made a move on her!

Has she ever had a boyfriend?

Well, no, but—

Oh my god...I don't want to hurt her!

Maybe that's why you need to tell her.
Since she's your best friend, it might be good to clear things up.
So, how did you know you were gay?
I always felt different—especially in middle school.
When other guys started crushing on girls, I realized I was crushing on guys.
How do you know you're not bi?
"I kissed girls during party games—it was no big thrill.
"But then one time everybody dared me and this other boy to kiss."
"And...? Did you?"

"Oh yeah...you bet we kissed.

"Everybody laughed like it was hilarious.
"But with that kiss I knew for sure what thrilled me: guys."

How about you? Ever kissed a guy?
Me...? No.
Ever wanted to?

Um...so... do you have...a boyfriend?
A boyfriend? In our puny fishbowl town? I wish.

It's hard to grow up different where different means people call you a freak.
Sometimes I feel like a fish out of water.

What's your family say? Have you told them?

My dad got sad and angry.
He said I would bring shame to our family.

Sorry I told him, but this is who I am.
He didn't want to talk about it after that.

And your mom?

She died when I was ten.
I'm really sorry.

Thanks. I still miss her some-times. Know what I mean?
Yeah, I do. What happened to her—if you don't mind?

No, I don't mind. She and my dad were in a car crash—
Hit by a drunk driver.
My dad survived but uses a wheelchair.
Life's never been easy after Mom died.
I help Dad out with our tourist lodge.
There's always something that needs fixing.
To him, that includes me.
Ha-ha!
Didn't you say your mom's scared of you getting near water?
Yeah, don't tell her!
She scared you might melt?

Not exactly melt. She's scared 'cause...
I'm a half-orphan, same as you. When I was a baby, my dad drowned.

Sorry, didn't know.

It's okay. My ma is like both a mom and dad.
Sometimes I barely have room to breathe around her.
I can relate.

What do you think she'd say if she knew about you?
I don't know. She's all I've got.

Did you know that the ocean once covered this entire desert?
Now the water is deep beneath us.
A whole fluid world...
Bubbling up...
And breaking through the surface.
Isn't water the coolest thing?
Sometimes I go to Hot Springs Park, next to our lodge, and watch the water for hours—

I think about life...how I got here...where I'm going...
Thanks.
I wondered why you always wear long sleeves.
Maria's the only friend I've ever let see my arms.
All my life I've felt like there's something wrong with me.
But my ma says it's a birthmark— she's a nurse, so...
Does it freak you out?
No, it's like a tattoo. I like it.
How far up does it go?
RUMBLE RUMBLE
Um, I can show you, if you want—

KRAK
Um, you want to see something even cooler?
Wow! How's it do that?
I'm not sure.
My ma says it has to do with my skin's electrical field.
You know how you said you feel like a fish out of water?
Me, too— except I'm an electric eel!

Can I touch it? Or will I get a shock?

KRAK
You can try.

Weird, huh?
No, I think it's awesome.

We should probably head back.
Probably.

Seriously, we don't want to get caught if it floods.

I'm a strong swimmer. I'll protect you.

KRRSH

Whoa, shit!

FWOOOSH

Gah!

Oomph!

Are you crazy? No way am I leaving you!

The story continues in
you brought me the ocean
On sale June 2020